Robert Williams Buchanan

Wayside Posies

Original Poems of the Country Life

Robert Williams Buchanan

Wayside Posies
Original Poems of the Country Life

ISBN/EAN: 9783337408299

Printed in Europe, USA, Canada, Australia, Japan

Cover: Foto ©Andreas Hilbeck / pixelio.de

More available books at **www.hansebooks.com**

WAYSIDE POSIES:

ORIGINAL POEMS OF THE COUNTRY LIFE.

EDITED BY

ROBERT BUCHANAN.

PICTURES

BY

G. J. PINWELL, J. W. NORTH, AND FREDERICK WALKER.

ENGRAVED BY

THE BROTHERS DALZIEL.

"There are flowers along the peasant's path
That kings might stoop to pull."
Old Song.

LONDON :
GEORGE ROUTLEDGE AND SONS,
BROADWAY, LUDGATE HILL.
1867.

PREFACE.

———

WHEN I was first requested to undertake the task of selecting the following poems, I had no idea that good verses were so scarce; but I have gathered together the best submitted to me by men both unknown and known, and (while including some little pieces of my own) have made all alike anonymous, that the unknown men might meet unprejudiced judgments. The singer of the terse and stirring rhyme called 'Reaping' is quite a new man, but he will soon (I anticipate) send out his voice from higher ground.

R. B.

London,
        November, 1866.

CONTENTS.

•

ILLUSTRATIONS.

———

ILLUSTRATIONS.

ILLUSTRATIONS.

THE SHADOW.

O, WILLOW FARM looks fine
  In the happy Summer days,
And the green trees all around
  Look golden in the haze;
The birds sing everywhere,
  And the flowers bloom once again,
And there's sweetness in the air,—
  But there's bitterness with men.

The Farm looks snug and old,
  But the slain birds on the wall,
And the cruel men who kill,
  Make me angry with it all;
The cows upon the mead
  Would be pleasant to mine eye,
But I sicken, as they lead
  The little calf to die.

There's something in it all
  That seems to spoil my joy,
I feel my heart grow chill,
  Though I am but a boy:
The world looks full of song,
  Of sweetness, once again,
But somehow all seems wrong
  Through the cruelty of men.

Why should the singing birds
  Fall by the fowler's gun?
Why should the young lambs die,
  When life has just begun?
O, all the world I see
  Would be fresh and free and fair,
Did not men's crueltie
  Put a shadow everywhere!

3

THE BIT O' GARDEN.

THE bit o' garden's tidier now than ever 't was before;
The fruit trees trim, and all in bloom, and roses at the door,
Aye, all looks sweet—'t is summer-time—the garden plots are bright,
And my old man is busy there from morning until night;
Yet here, indoors, 't is weary now, and all for Lizzie's sake,—
But for the bit o' garden ground, my old man's heart would break.

For Lizzie was his darling pride, the treasure of his life:
'T was even pain to think our girl might leave to be a wife;
And now, though even that was sad, 't is bitterer, sorer pain
To think she should be here and know we cannot part again;
And then to think the bitterest sound at our fireside should be
The crying of the little one upon our daughter's knee!

Oh! weary was the waiting while our daughter was away;
The bit o' garden ground ran wild; we listened night and day;
And then that night when all the town was lying in its rest,
We saw her standing at the door, her baby at her breast,
And my old man leapt up, and cried, and kissed her on the cheek,
And the kiss was bitterer to bear than words the tongue can speak!

And all the shame is put away: there's peace upon her face;
But though we love to hear her laugh, the laugh seems out o' place:
She is the dearest daughter still that ever father had,
But there is quiet in the house, and, somehow, all seems sad,—
'T is weary now with over-love, and all for Lizzie's sake:
But for the bit o' garden ground, my old man's heart would break!

AT THE GRINDSTONE;

OR, A HOME VIEW OF THE BATTLE-FIELD.

GRIND, Billie, grind!   And so the war's begun?
  Flash, bayonets! cannons, call! dash down their pride!
If I was younger, I would grip a gun,
  And die a-field, as better men have died:
I'd face three Frenchmen, lad, and feel no fear,
With this old knife that we are grinding here!

Why, I'm a kind of radical, and saw
  Some fighting in the riots long ago;
But, Lord, am I the sort of chap to draw
  A sword against old Mother England?   No!
England for me, with all her errors, still—
I hate them foreigners, and always will!

There was our Johnie, now!—as kind a lad
  As ever grew in England; fresh and fair!
To see him in his regimentals clad,
  With honest rosy cheeks and yellow hair,
Was something, Billy, worthy to be seen;
But Johnie's gone—murdered at seventeen!

None of your fighting sort, but mild and shy,
  Soft-hearted, full of wench-like tenderness,
Without the heart, indeed, to hurt a fly;
  But fond, you see, of music and of dress:
We could not hold him in, dear lad, and so
He heard the fife, and would a-soldiering go.

And it was pleasant for a time to see
  Johnie, our little drummer, go and come,
Holding his head up, proudly, merrily,
  Happy with coat o' red, and hat, and drum.
That was in peace; but war broke out one day,
And Johnie's regiment was called away.

AT THE GRINDSTONE.

He went! he went! he could not choose but go!
  And me and my old woman wearied here:
We knew that men must fall and blood must flow,
  But still had many a thought to lighten fear:
Those Russian men could never be so bad
As kill or harm so very small a lad;

A lad that should have been at school or play!
  A little baby in a coat o' red!
What! touch our little Johnie? No, not they!
  Why, they had little ones themselves, we said.
Billie, the little lad we loved so well
Was slain among the very first that fell!

Mark that! A bullet from a murderous gun
  Singled him out, and struck him to the brain:
He fell—our boy, our joy, our little one—
  His bright hair dark with many a bloody stain,
His clammy hands clenched tight, his eyes o' brown
Looking through smoke and fire to Stamford town!

What, call that war! to slay a helpless child
  Who never, never hurt a living thing!
Butchered, for what we know, too, while he smiled
  On the strange light all round him, wondering!
Grind, Billie, grind! call, cannons! bayonets, thrust!
Would we were grinding all our foes to dust!

Bah! Frenchman, Turk, or Russian—all alike!
  All eaten up with slaughter, sin, and slavery!
Little care they what harmless hearts they strike—
  They murder little lads, and call it bravery!
Down with them when they cross our path, I say:
Give me old England's manhood and fair play!

8

SHADOW AND SUBSTANCE.

THE sun is bright in the meadow,
  The Spring flowers blow,
Nell stands by the stream, and her shadow
  Glimmers below ;
And I try to muster the daring
  To creep more near,
And whisper the passion past bearing
  Into her ear.

Her eyelids droop while she fishes,
  Her eyes look down !—
But while I whispered my wishes,
  If Nell should frown,
I think I should turn to self-slaughter
  As something sweet,
And, embracing her shade in the water,
  Die at her feet !

AFLOAT ON THE STREAM.

I.

THE town upon the river-side,
Wherein my love and I abide,
  Keeps many a hungry home :
Beyond those clouds the ocean's lips
Are shady with the white-winged ships,
  And bright with flying foam.

AFLOAT ON THE STREAM.

Here the black barges darken down
Into the suburb, where the town
   Begins with lane and street;
Here are few flowers save human ones,
That blossom sickly: slowly runs
   The river at their feet.

Here, where the darkened sunlights fall
On haggard wives and children small,
   The river singing flows,
And, sometimes brightening unaware,
Flashing its silver in the air,
   It broadens as it goes.

And oft we launch our little boat,
And sweetly, quietly we float
   Toward the gates of morn;
Away from city, smoke, and sin,
Unto the solitude wherein
   The happy stream is born.

AFLOAT ON THE STREAM.

II.

Hither the sunshine cometh not,
But leafy branches shade the spot
  Where sleeps the baby stream ;
And here with folded wings Love lies,—
We feel his breathing, and our eyes
  Meet in a happy dream.

There, looking down upon its face,
We watch the water in the place
   From whence it singing flows,
And picture sweetly, while we rest,
A little Naiad in a nest,
   Where the wild lily blows.

Yonder there spreads the harvest scene,
The slanted sheaves, where gleaners glean
   And haymakers carouse :
Here, floating, dreaming, at our will,
We hear the water, feel the still
   Eye-music of green boughs.

And all around are glimpses sweet
Of sunny slopes where white flocks bleat ;
   Of many a quiet glade,
Where all is coolness, though above
The sunlight faints on clouds, that move
   Slowly and cast no shade.

AFLOAT ON THE STREAM.

III.

Downward at eventide go we :
The river, broadening to the sea,
  Sighs as we sit and muse ;

The flitter-mice around us cry,
And far away the sunset sky
  Takes melancholy hues.

AFLOAT ON THE STREAM.

Past little villages we go,
With quaint old gable-ends that glow
   Still in the sunset's fire;
And gliding through the shadows still,
Oft notice, with a lover's thrill,
   The peeping of a spire.

Then silent in our little boat,
With downward-drooping eyes we float:
   All human joy and grief
Are hushed around us at this hour;
The silence flutters like a flower,
   And closes leaf by leaf.

The heart beats quick, the bosom sighs;
Westward we gaze, and in our eyes
   More pensive love-thoughts dawn;
For, from the amber sky afar,
The twilight of the lover's star
   Is delicately drawn.

SCHOOL.

I SAUNTERED where the town and country meet,
Where Art and Nature battle for the street,
Where, ere the stones had vanished from my foot,
The grass laughed up at me a gay salute.
In leafy contiguity I heard
The mellow note of some love-brooding bird;
And nearer still I heard a droning noise
Come from a hive of bees or school of boys,
But which I could not tell, until my eye
Lighted upon a porch, as butterfly
Lights on a kingdom of all-mingled bloom,
Wherein the flowers breathe out their beauteous doom,
And fill the air with souls. To that flower-cell
I leaned my ear, as to a humming shell,
And heard the moan as of a fairy sea
Far in the dim domain of mystery.
Then growing bolder, I advanced a pace
Into the trellised porch, and saw the place;
And, lo! as I do live, a little school,
Wherein an easy dame kept easy rule,
And learned, as well as taught, the way to know.
About her sat, but in no formal row,
Her little students, serious, but unfrightened.
Surely, I thought, this is a school enlightened,
Where neither word of wrath nor lash descends
To harden knowledge unto hateful ends;
Where rule is quietly taught and quickly learned,—
Things apprehended, if not quite discerned;
And where bright youth is lifted to a height
From which he sees each glorious height on height—
Those starry souls by whose effulgent breath
The world is snatched from chaos, man from death.

A pleasant school—a pleasant sight for eye
That loveth spots where nothing seems to die;
Where winds are soft, flowers sweetly bloom, and man
Fits like a star into dear Nature's plan,
And wins by truth and unreposing duty
The throne of wisdom and the crown of beauty.

ON THE SHORE.

WHEREFORE so cold, O day,
That gleamest far away
O'er the dim line where mingle heaven and ocean,
While fishing-boats lie nestled in the grey,
And the small wave gleams in its shoreward motion?
Wherefore so cold, so cold?
O say, dost thou behold
A face o'er which the rock-weed droopeth sobbing,
A face just stirrèd in a sea-cave old
By the green water's throbbing?

Wherefore, O fisherman,
So full of care and wan,
This weary, weary morning shoreward flying,
While, stooping downward darkly, dost thou scan
That which below thee in thy boat is lying?
Wherefore so full of care?
What dost thou shoreward bear,
Caught in thy net's moist meshes, as a token?
Ah, can it be the ring of golden hair
Whereby my heart is broken?

Wherefore so still, O sea,
That washest wearilie
Under the lamp lit in the fisher's dwelling,
Holding the secret of thy deeps from me,
Whose heart would break so sharply at the telling?
Wherefore so still, so still?
Say, in thy sea-cave chill,
Floats she forlorn with foam-bells round her breaking,
While the wet fisher lands and climbs the hill
To hungry babes awaking?

THE SWALLOWS.

I.

O CHURCHYARD in the shady gloom,
   What charm to please hast thou,
That, seated on a broken tomb,
   I muse so oft as now?
The dreary autumn woodland whispers nigh,
And in the distant lanes the village urchins cry.

Thou holdest in thy sunless land
   Nought I have seen or known,
No lips I ever kissed, no hand
   That ever clasped mine own ;
And all is still and dreary to the eye,—
The broken tombs, dark walls, the patch of cloudy sky.

And to the murmur that mine ears
   Catch from the distant lanes,
Dimming mine eyes with dreamy tears,
   Slow, low, my heart refrains,
And the live grass creeps up from thy dead bones,
And crawls, with slimy stains, over thy grey grave-stones.

The cries keep on, the minutes pass,
   Mine eyes are on the ground,
The silent many-fingered grass
   Winds round, and round, and round :
I seem to see it live, and stir, and wind,
And gaze until a weight is heavy on my mind.

THE SWALLOWS.

II.

O churchyard in the shady gloom,
    What charm to please hast thou,
That, seated on a broken tomb,
    I muse so oft as now ?
Haply because I learn, with sad content,
How small a thing can make the whole world different !

Among thy grave-stones worn and old,
    A sad sweet hour I pass,
Where thickest from thy sunless mould
    Upsprings the sickly grass ;
For, though the earth holds no sweet-smelling flower,
The swallows build their nests up in thy square grey tower.

While, burthened by the life we bear,
    The dull and creeping woe,
The mystery, the pain, the care,
    I watch thy grasses grow,
Sighing, I look to the dull autumn skies,
And, lo ! my heart is cheered, and tears are in mine eyes.

For here, where stillness, death, and dream,
    Brood over creeping things,
Over mine eyes with quick bright gleam
    Shine little flashing wings,
And a strange wonder takes thy shady air,
And the deep life I breathe seems sweetened unaware !

HOPE.

Fly, Hope, and do not linger on the wing!
   Fly to the lover, cloudy with his woe:
Dawn on him like a tender morn of Spring,
   And let him hear thy cheering streamlets flow;
Uplift the shadowy curtain from his eye,
And show him where thy starry kingdoms lie.

Fly, Hope, unto the maiden, blind with tears
   For one belovèd but no longer true:
Give her the silent valour of the years,
   Whose rectitude no falsehood can undo;
Give her the Bridegroom of that gracious clime
Which knows not change of love nor lapse of time.

Fly, Hope, unto the student, poor and pale :
  Warm the cold squalor of his little room ;
Goad him to glory; yet, if he must fail,
  Content him with the wretched-righteous doom ;
If foes belie him, or false friendship frown,
Give him the power to live the liars down.

Fly, Hope, to stony pillows, where the poor
  Groan out their lives on scant parochial cheer :
Send them a dream that they may half endure
  Their one last horror of a pauper's bier ;
Lay thy soft fingers on their hollow eyes,
And mix thy balm with their departing sighs.

Fly, Hope, unto the husbandman : make morn
  Cheer his sad fancy as he jogs a-field ;
Glance from the heavens a glory on the corn,
  That he may think whence comes the goodliest yield ;
Give him the thinking soul and seeing eye,
To find the Edens where true harvests lie.

Fly, Hope, to voyagers on far-off seas,
  Dashed by the storm or idling in the calm :
Soothe the rough billows, raise the lingering breeze ;
  Flood their keen memories with the home-breathed psalm ;
Tickle their palms, as if a baby's hand
Were stretched to them from out their native land.

Fly, Hope, to wrinkled Ninety with his staff ;
  And, if you can no more prolong his days,
Straighten his limbs in fancy; let him quaff
  The cup that kindles Heaven's immortal blaze—
That other morn, the dawn on death's sweet night,
Sunned with all visions of celestial light.

SPRING.

The light of the season awakes,
  The warm wind softens the cold,
And the lady laburnum shakes
  Her treacherous tresses of gold.

The cuckoo-flower sprinkles abroad
  Her stars of purple and pink,
And the dark green cresses are strewed
  On the wandering streamlet's brink.

O violet, why do you speak
  Of the one sad Spring long by?
O wind, that circles my cheek,
  Have you no voice but a sigh?

From the sheep half hid on the hill
  Comes the soft low bleat as of yore;
And the sound of the trickling rill
  Bears the music it always bore.

Yet why will they tell and tell
  Only of bygone things—
Like the boom of an ocean shell
  That only of ocean sings?

They are the same—each one—
  The hill, the vale, and the stream,
And the white of the mid-day sun
  That softens them into a dream.

But away where the glory glares
  On the broad old mulberry tree,
A little white stone declares
  What has altered them all to me.

28

THE JOURNEY'S END.

The man lay down and dreamed a dream of old.
Forgotten was the sultry heat of noon,
The long, long journey, and the tirèd limbs;
Forgotten, too, the stealthy fire that sucked
The life-blood of his heart from day to day.
And, lo! a village by the sunny Loire,
With trees down-sloping to the river's blue,
Above, upon the height, a ruined tower,
And out beyond the houses a square plain,
Dotted with stones and crosses of black iron,
Children are playing there, scarce knowing how
Or why came all these yellow wreaths, and plots
Of little flowers, and, in the crosses, squares
Glass-covered, with the Virgin's face inside.
The children leave the place: he sees them go,
This way and that way over all the world,
Through rain, and wind, and torrid heat, and snow.
But one of all returns; and as he looks—
O Heaven! a coldness falls upon his heart—
Surely he knows the man, dim-eyed, forlorn,
Who stumbles forward with a little cry,
And falls, face downward, on the yielding grass.

The people of the farm-yard cluster round,
And with mute, curious eyes behold the pair,—
The English wife, asleep, her babe held tight,
The man, with bronzed and haggard face, a stripe
Of tinsel on his brow, and his lithe form
Clad in fantastic costume. Suddenly
His weary head falls over with a sigh
And twitching of the mouth. They wait and look.
There is no further motion of the face,
No further heaving of the narrow chest.
One, fearing, takes the lean and withered hand,
And straightway lets it drop.—The man is dead.
And still his wife sleeps on, her child close wrapped
And folded to her breast; and they around
Ask, without speech, who first shall bid her wake?

REAPING.

Up, mortal, and act, while the angel of light
   Melts the shadows before and behind thee!
Shake off the soft dreams that encumber thy might,
   And burst the fool's fetters that bind thee!

Soars the skylark—soar thou ; leaps the stream—do thou leap ;
  Learn from Nature the splendour of action :
Plough, harrow, and sow, or thou never shalt reap ;
  Faithful deed brings divine benefaction.

The red sun has rolled himself into the blue,
  And lifted the mists from the mountain ;
The young hares are feasting on nectar of dew,
  The stag cools his lips in the fountain,
The blackbird is piping within the dim elm,
  The river is sparkling and leaping,
The wild bee is fencing the sweets of his realm,
  And the mighty-limbed reapers are reaping.

To Spring comes the budding ; to Summer, the blush ;
  To Autumn, the happy fruition ;
To Winter, repose, meditation, and hush ;
  But to man, every season's condition :
He buds, blooms, and ripens in action and rest,
  As thinker, and actor, and sleeper ;
Then withers and wavers, chin drooping on breast,
  And is reaped by the hand of a Reaper.

KING PIPPIN.

KING PEPIN was the King of France ;
　A little dapper king was he,
And yet he had a son as big
　As ever reigned on land or sea,
Long-legged, long-armed, of mighty strength,
　Was kingly-minded, brave, and free :
But what's King Pepin unto you ?
　And what is Charlemagne to me ?

KING PIPPIN.

I have a better king than both;
  A pretty little man is he:
Not *Pep*, but *Pippin* is his name—
  His kingdom is an apple tree.
He wears an ever-gracious smile,
  And all the monarch fires his e'e:
A kingly head, a queenly heart—
  Oh, that's the golden king for me!

Just see him in the Spring-time clear,
  When star-buds fire the apple tree;
He dances round it like a fay,
  And makes the orchard ring with glee;
And when soft Summer, leafily green,
  Breathes daisies in the furrowed lea,
King Pippin, on a bed of blooms,
  Finds heaven beneath the royal tree.

But when old tawny Autumn comes,
  With apples laughing on the tree,
King Pippin sits beneath and sings,
  'I am your king, come down to me!'
Then up the ladder mounts and sits
  Cheek-by-jowl with his subjects free,
Who, blushing, shout with one acclaim,
  'Hail! Pippin, King of the Apple Tree!'

And when the apples are gathered in,
   The king—a royal judge is he—
Receives them from a beauteous maid,
   Who brings them on her bended knee.
And he assigns their righteous doom
   Where'er their various merits lie,—
Sends this to rot, gives that to eat,
   The rest to pudding, pig, or pie.

Oh, Pippin is a worthy king;
   An apple-cheekèd king is he:
I love him more than all the kings
   That wear old crowns beyond the sea.
I would not give his little thumb
   For those grim-headed emperors three,
Whose legs are twined about the world,
   As if it were *their* apple tree.

Sing Pippin hey! sing Pippin ho!
   The best of all the kings is he!
Nor thought he stabs, nor speech he chokes,
   Nor steals the bairnie from our knee;
He lets us think, he lets us speak,
   And sport beneath his apple tree:
I bless him once, I bless him twice,
   I bless him everlastingly!

BY THE DOVE-COT.

THE place around her is enchanted;
Sweetly she pauses, troubled, haunted,
  For all the air seems full of love,—
Music of billing and of cooing,
Music of little winged things wooing
  Around her, under, and above.

With rosy ears and tingling fingers,
Like Venus 'mid her doves she lingers,
  Her bosom rich with honied things;
The gladness round her has no measure,
The warm air palpitates for pleasure,
  Troubled by white and waving wings.

What fitter time to creep and woo her,
When light and sound and love thrill through her,
  Stirring her gentle blood like wine?
All gentle things that round her hover
Conspire, O happy, happy lover,
  To honey her sweet mouth for thine.

THE NUTTING.

I LOVE my pretty cousin Kate,
   Altho' I scarcely reach her shoulder,
Altho' my age is only eight,
   And she is more than seven years older.

THE NUTTING.

Though she is tall, she's sweet and free,
   Though she looks proud, no face is fonder,
And Kate is wild and glad like me,
   When nutting in the woods we wander!

Fine are the woods by Clover Heath
   In golden weather such as this is—
She cracks me nuts with her sweet teeth,
   And gives them me with kindly kisses.

And by the stream, that sings a tune,
   Beside sweet Kate I musing tarry,
And eat the nuts, and count how soon
   I shall be big enough to marry.

Oh, fine it is through branches brown
   To scramble, laughing, shouting, tearing,
Sweet Kitty in her cotton gown,
   And I for scratches little caring.

I wish for evermore that she
   May be my mate in woods like this is,
And laugh, and crack the nuts for me,
   And while I eat them give me kisses.

Kate is the only wife I'll wed;
   She's blithe and bold, and greedy never;
That Kate loves me is clear, I've said,
   And I'll be true to Kate for ever!

THE VISIONS OF A CITY TREE.

THE city roars around my feet
   In squares, and lanes, and alleys,
On every side my trunk a street—
   So different from the valleys
Where, through the alders bathed in green,
The streamlet's sunny lights are seen.

The men look up and think that I
   Lend sweetness to their riches:
I'd rather let my branches lie
   O'er limpid country ditches,
Where the blue speedwells softly blow
To grace the rivulet below.

I weary of their fight for gold,
   Their ceaseless toil and hurry:
Alas! my topmost twigs behold
   The emerald hills of Surrey,
And I would fain be there to see
The sun chase shadows on the lea.

From morn till night the city hums
   With dim of wheel and hammer,
And shriek of railway whistle comes
   To pierce the giant clamour.
And ever on and on they flow—
Those eager, eddying crowds below.

But in the night-time I am blessed
  With many a lovelier vision
Than ever soothed a maiden's rest
  With dreams of lands Elysian:
Lo, pale Capella and red Mars
Crown me with diadem of stars!

I watch the sunset's latest dart
  Pale in the clear, cool even,
Till the white moon becomes the heart
  Of the violet of heaven;
And then I watch this glorious flower
Grow lovelier through each silent hour.

And yet I would not leave the town,
  Men look on me so kindly!
Sometimes I think that far, far down
  Within their hearts, they blindly
Bestow unconscious thanks on me,
And bless the green of the old tree!

And so I am content to wait
  Within this toil and hurry;
Perhaps I am of better estate
  Than my brethren down in Surrey:
Men love me that my branches bright
Touch the dull town with country light.

THE GOOSE.

O ELSIE CARR, that single goose
  Is worse than all your twenty:
'T was surely hatched when screws were loose
  And addled eggs were plenty.

It waddles out, it waddles in,
  With one eternal cackle,
As if 't were egg'd to make such din
  By eggs still held in shackle.

Go, Elsie, yonder stalks the wretch,
  Majestically going,
With step undaunted, neck on stretch,
  Big, blusterous, and blowing;
Yet, Elsie, with that willow bough
  Be tender, O be human!
A goose is but a goose, you know,
  And not a man or woman.

Well, shake your fist to save the rod,
  But when was fool affrighted?
A goose will cackle at a god,
  And clap his wings delighted.

THE GOOSE.

And, Elsie, think I am a seer
  Of power and penetration,
When of the cackling that you hear
  I offer this translation:

Stay, mortal! since I be a goose
  With little understanding,
Why am I not beneath abuse
  Of one so all-commanding?
My web foot came from Heaven, like thine,
  And Heaven knows best the reason;
Your language possibly is fine,
  Yet cackling can't be treason.

O ye that waste your precious lives
  In idle talks and tattles,
Cutting your throats with golden knives,
  Pleased with your gilded rattles;
Shouting at Heaven in your joys,
  Shrieking in your bereavement,
How very mighty is your noise!
  How little your achievement!

Ye wear your lives in fruitless things;
  Chagrin deforms your features;
Ye wish to soar—ye cry for wings,
  Yet mock us wingèd creatures;
Your boasted feats are thin and poor,
  Howe'er the flash may blind us;
While, when WE *cackle, we are sure*
  To leave an EGG *behind us!*

GLEN-OONA.

AND is there still joy in the vale of Glen-Oona?
  Oh, sings there the lark as it sings not elsewhere?
Is life still a dream in the vale of Glen-Oona?
  Hushed and sweet as the breath of the clear mountain air?

Thirty years since I went from the vale of Glen-Oona,
  Thirty years since we parted in anger and pride;
With a heart full of darkness I went from Glen-Oona,
  For the petulant hope of my boyhood had died.

And I cursed her who dwelt in the vale of Glen-Oona,
  And I turned from her face that was false through her tears,
And I fled far away from the vale of Glen-Oona
  Till my sorrow was dulled by the ministrant years.

But memory loved the clear vale of Glen-Oona,
  And graced it and gave it the glory of dawn,
Till there grew up another and rarer Glen-Oona,
  More beautiful far than the one that was gone.

And now, once again, I look down on Glen-Oona,
  Asleep in the sunshine that falls from the hill;
But this is a colder and greyer Glen-Oona,
  And my heart, unresponsive, refuses to thrill.

Oh, where is the olden and golden Glen-Oona
  I saw when the sea-winds spoke softly and low?
I would I could turn from this vale of Glen-Oona
  To the vale that I loved in the years long ago.

47

THE ISLAND BEE.

A RHYME.

FAR from his island bowers
  Daily he wanders,
Kissing the virgin flowers
  Of the mainlanders.

Far o'er the lonely wild
  White the stream foameth;
There this undaunted Gael
  Fearlessly roameth.

Over the mighty ben
  Into the corry,
Piping he sweeps agen
  On his sweet foray.

Where the sweet homestead peers,
  Singing he cometh;
Round the farm urchin's ears
  Terribly hummeth;

Brushing with pinion sweet,
  Hydromel-laden,
The dew-drops around the feet
  Of the farm maiden.

Then as o'er eave and vane
  Hovers the swallow,
And o'er the western main
  Stoops red Apollo,

Homeward, by ocean's brink,
  Briskly he urges,
Where the blind cockles blink
  Under the surges.

Over the strait he flies
  To the green islands,
Bearing about his thighs
  Spoils from the nigh lands.

All the drones hum with glee,
  " Hail to the Raider,
Claymored and tartan'd Bee,
  Matchless invader !

" Bravely gone, safely come,
  Chieftain unconquered !
Give him a Highland hum !
  Give him a tankard ! "

Then to the hive they flee,
  Red, black, and yellow,
Where he gets three times three—
  Jolly good fellow !

A VESPER HYMN.

SWEET is the little scented spot
   Where we have dwelt for many a year,
And sweet still seems our wedded lot,
   Now the grey sleeping-time is near;

A VESPER HYMN.

Chill lies the dew—the moments fleet—
The shadows lengthen at our feet—
  The quiet of the Night is near us now;
Yet peaceful is the Night, though Light be sweet :—
  This is God's truth, I trow.

We have been happy many a day,
  We have been weary many more;
We have been sad—we have been gay;
  Life has been sweet—life has been sore;
And oft, in sorrows manifold,
The Light from heaven seemed cruel cold,
  And Death looked hitherward with pitiless brow;
But Death looks very mildly on the old :—
  This is God's truth, I trow.

We are so old and sleepy-eyed,
  We scarcely heed the things we see,—
To rest together side by side
  Will be relief to thee and me !
Our eyes are dim, our heads are white,
We can no longer bear the Light,
  Our children drink the joy we tire of now,
While still and sweet and holy comes the Night :—
  This is God's truth, I trow.

RAIN.

Now, breathing up from beds of balm,
  The Angel of the Spring appears,
With wings that droop in pensive calm,
  And eyes that startle light from tears ;
And where she goes she leaves behind
  Her footprints green in wood and lane,
And in her changeful path the wind
  Blows the wild shadows of the rain.

Oh, watch them blown from hill to hill,
  O'er silent streams and breezy downs,
From thorp to thorp, from vill to vill,
  And over solitary towns.
Oh, watch them go, Oh, watch them blow,
  With silvery gleams of light between,
While branches grow, and waters flow,
  And woods and lawns grow dewy green !

Oh, dark and still across the ground
  The melancholy shadows fly,
And where they pass, with weeping sound,
  Unseen the Angel passes by.
Yet often, while the sweet show'rs flow,
  A glory flits from place to place,
And, girdled by the beauteous Bow,
  Comes a strange glimmer of her face !

STAINLEY FERRY.

THIS is Stainley Ferry:
   Here we met and parted—
Meeting, we were merry,
   Parting, broken-hearted.
She came—she went away—
   I kissed her—she was gone:
Unchanged at all, from day to day
   The river is flowing on.

Still looks Stainley Ferry,
  By the peaceful river:
Ever-changing faces
  Come and go for ever;
Never one may stay—
  They flit—they fade—are gone;
While still unchanged, from day to day
  The river is flowing on.

Why by Stainley Ferry
  Muse I like a lover?
Love must come and vanish,
  Youth is quickly over.
Sweet lips turn to clay,
  Pleasure must begone,
While still unchanged, from day to day
  The river is flowing on.

NORLAN FARM.

PLEASANT lie the woods round Norlan
  When the leaf is on the tree :
Here, beside the woods of Norlan,
  Here he kissed and trysted me.
Follow him, follow him, wind from Norlan,
  Wheresoe'er he be !

Here we met and here we parted,
  In the evening of the year ;
Happy sounds were heard from Norlan,
  And the wood birds whistled near.
Follow him, follow him, sounds from Norlan,
  Whisper in his ear !

Flocks and herds were murm'ring round us ;
  Calm was all the eye could trace ;
In the west the mild sun, sinking,
  Smiled upon the peaceful place.
Follow him, sounds and sights from Norlan,
  With my voice and face !

Blow upon him, wind from Norlan,
  Though in mists of fight he be ;
Flash, O peaceful sights of Norlan,
  On my soldier's memorie !
Living or dying, Norlan, Norlan,
  Let him think of me !

THE OLD CART.

THROUGH many a year of troubles and of joys,
　　Strong friend and faithful has this old cart been!
Ah, if it just for once could find a voice!
　　Could chatter of the things that it has seen!

THE OLD CART.

Many a pretty burthen has it carried,
  And heard the talk of many a friendly tongue.
How long ago I drove down to be married!
  And this old cart was new, and I was young!

In this old cart right often, long ago,
  My Bessie drove to market in her bloom;
And, ah! in this old cart, so sad, so slow,
  I drove her down to put her in her tomb.
And now, while I am close to sleeping with her,
  Useless and old, here our old friend is flung;
And I am tired of trudging hither, thither,
  And this old cart was new when I was young.

Old cart, just fit for firewood,—spent, like me!
  Old limbs of mine, no longer strong or fleet!
Yet what sweet girls have sat upon this knee,
  What pretty shapes have warmed that ancient seat!
All's over now! our spell of work is wrought!
  And here we linger newer things among,
One fit for firewood, t' other fit for nought;
  And this old cart was new when I was young.

KITTY MORRIS.

KITTY MORRIS has made me sad,—
Though she is a woman, and I am a lad.

I think of her beauty in a dream :
The thought of her lips is like drinking cream.

Kitty's breath, when she passes me,
Leaves scent like the bloom of an apple tree.

The wave of her dress is witching sweet,
Shining and thrilling like waving wheat.

KITTY MORRIS.

Why should Kitty trouble me so ?—
She is in love with a tall fellòw!

To me she is so merry and kind,
That she leaves a sense of despair behind.

Kitty has ever a smile for me,
Yet can be sharp with a man, you see!

Would she were cruel and hard to please :
With me, alas! she is ever at ease.

She laughs if I press her finger-tips;
She would not scream if I kissed her lips.

With me she has neither shame nor fear,
Yet blushes bright when a man is near!

O, might I be the dress she wears!
Or the mat she kneels on to wash the stairs!

Would I were one of her hens or ducks!
Ay! or the very goose she plucks!

Would I were the pudding she makes,
Tasted so daintily while it bakes!

Would I were the little boot,
Kissing the curve of her dainty foot!

Anything rather than feel so sad,—
See Kitty a woman, and I but a lad!

A VAGRANT'S SONG.

O THOU who, with a giftless hand,
  Dost early toil and late
To scare the wild bird from thy land,
  The beggar from thy gate,
Up with thy scarecrows when they come,
  The world is wide, I trust :
The wandering bird will find a crumb,
  The wandering man a crust.

Preserve thy proper heritage,
  Respect thy little creed,
Flourish content within thy cage,
  And dully chirp and feed ;
While wild and free we go and come,
  And wander as we must,
The wandering bird will find a crumb,
  The wandering man a crust.

Content within thy narrow space,
  There let thy wings be furled ;
Con o'er each old familiar face,
  And think thou feel'st the world ;
What care the shapes that go and come,
  Begrimed and dark with dust ?—
The wandering bird will find a crumb,
  The wandering man a crust.

A VAGRANT'S SONG.

Yet, surely, wheresoe'er we roll,
　　How deep soe'er we grieve,
We feel a motion of man's soul
　　Thou dost but half perceive;
Our spirits, neither blind nor dumb,
　　Between no bars are thrust,
And wandering birds will find a crumb,
　　And wandering men a crust.

Ay! while we roam we see full plain,
　　Not merely grass and clod—
A world that, like a thing in pain,
　　Feels the strange gaze of God;
Under that gaze we go and come,
　　In wonder, yet in trust,
For wandering birds will find a crumb,
　　And wandering men a crust.

SUMMER STORM.

WE quarrelled this morning, my wife and I—
We were out of temper and scarce knew why,
    Tho' the cause was trivial—common;
But to look at us then, you'd have sworn that we both
Were a couple of enemies cruel and wroth,
    Not a wedded man and woman.

Wife, like a tragedy queen in a play,
Tossed her sweet little head in as spiteful a way
    As so gentle a woman was able;
She clenched her lips with a sneer and frown;
While I, being rougher, stamped up and down,
    Like a careless groom in a stable.

You'd have thought us the bitterest (seeing us then)
Of little women and little men,
    You'd have laughed at our spite and passion,
And would never have dreamed that a storm like this
Would be rainbowed out into tears with a kiss,
    Till we talked in the old fond fashion.

The storm was over in less than an hour,
It was followed at once by a sunny shower,
    And that again by embraces;
Yet so little the meaning was understood
That we almost felt ashamed to be good,
    And wore a blush on our faces.

Then she, as a woman, much braver became,
And tried to bear the whole weight of the blame,
   By her kindness herself reproving ;
Then, seeing her humble and knowing her true,
I all at once became humble too,
   And very contrite and loving.

But, seeing me acting a humble part,
She laughed outright with a frolic heart—
   With as careless a laugh as Cupid ;
And the laughter echoed along my brain,
Till I almost felt in a passion again,
   And became quite stubborn and stupid.

And this was the time for her arms to twine
Around this stubbornest neck of mine
   Like the arms of a maid round a lover ;
And feeling them there with their love, you know,
I laughed quite a different laugh, and so
   The summer storm was over !

OUR LITTLE ONE.

ALL day long the house was glad
  With the patter of little happy feet;
Never was stranger's face so sad,
  But it brightened to see a thing so sweet:
Hither and thither all the day,
  Here did our little one laugh and leap,
Till his eyes grew dim as the world grew gray,
And in his little bed he lay,
  Tired, tired, and fast asleep.

But all the house is very still,
  The world looks awful beyond the door;
All is still, and all is chill,
  And our little one will wake no more.
Yet it does not seem that he is dead—
  His slumber does not seem so deep;
'Tis only dark because day has fled,
And he is lying on his bed,
  Tired, tired, and fast asleep.

Alas! he smiles as if he dreams!
  Can Death indeed be such as this?
He lies so prettily, it seems
  That I could wake him with a kiss.
'Tis like the nights that used to be—
  Only I wring my hands and weep,
And the night is very dark, and, see!
There on his little bed lies he,
  Tired, tired, and fast asleep.

AUTUMNAL SONG.

Now, dark and dry is piled the wheat,
The wine-press feels no stainèd feet,
    The white moon shrinks her sickle clear,
And voices of the air repeat,
    ' It is the evening of the year.'

AUTUMNAL SONG.

Why have I missed, while men have found?
Men smile that corn and wine abound,
   And children eat the ripened ear;
I gaze at them from barren ground:
   It is the evening of the year.

O Love! it seems but yesterday,
A child in fresh green fields I lay,
   And dreamt of thee where skies were clear;
But withered leaves bestrew my way:
   It is the evening of the year.

O Face that I have never seen!
Somewhere on earth with saddened mien
   Thou waitest, full of sober cheer;—
Come! where the reaper's foot hath been:
   It is the evening of the year.

Come to me, O my Love, my Fate,
Ere all be cold and desolate!
   Come!—I have sought thee far and near;
Come!—lest I wither while I wait:
   It is the evening of the year.

WINTER SONG.

WINTRY winds are calling,
  Wheresoe'er I go,
Dismally is falling
  The melancholy snow;

72

WINTER SONG.

Birds from off the bough
  Long have taken flight,
There is no singing now,
  And scant sun-light.
I weary for the old days,
  When all the world looked gay;
These are the cold days!
  Summer hath fled away!

Love, and peace, and gladness
  Stayed a little space;
Solitude and sadness
  Meet me in their place:
Love passed idly by,
  Soon was gladness flown,
Peace was last to fly—
  I am alone!
And I weary for the old days,
  And those who would not stay;
These are the cold days!
  Summer hath fled away!

Heart, hast thou a reason
  Thus to throb and yearn?
In the wintry season
  Why should he return?
In the wintry hours
  'Tis too late to gain
One who 'mid the flowers
  Would not remain;
And I weary for the old days,
  And one who would not stay;
These are the cold days!
  Summer hath fled away!

DOCTOR TOM.

Of all the doctors that there be,
Doctor Tom for my monie;
He came to cure the cow, you see,
And finished off by curing me!

Horses and cattle are his trade,
But he for finer things was made:
He understands a human case
Better than any one in the place.

For fret and trouble day and night,
Worry and fidget left and right,
Muddle and trouble everywhere,
Were growing more than I could bear.

A widow here I dwelt for years,
And life was full of frets and fears ;
The crops and flocks were growing small—
I could not manage things at all.

But Doctor with his cheery face
Brought better than physic to the place :
He came to keep the cow from harm,
And morn and night was at the farm.

At last he whispered in mine ear,
' You 're looking like a ghost, my dear !
But you shall soon be fresh and free
If you 'll entrust your case to me.'

DOCTOR TOM.

He found me willing, for I knew
That he was clever, strong, and true,
And, tho' the gossips spoke their thought,
I took the comfort that he brought.

At last, when several weeks had fled,
'It's time to finish the cure,' he said,
And round my waist his arm he threw,—
And married me before I knew!

The cow is milking down the dell,
The farm and flocks are doing well:
Was ever doctor half so clever?—
My complaint is gone for ever.

THE HEATH.

YONDER heath is a barren place,
But she lights it nightly with her face.

Common and bare the whole day thro',
It glitters by night with white moon-dew.

The brakes and bushes take form, and stir
Like gentle shapes, at the voice of her.

A charm is in the earth and air,
The winds sound wondrous, when she is there.

The pale stars cluster in the skies,
And gaze upon her with glistening eyes.

THE HEATH.

Charmèd and fair the heath has grown,
When I hie to meet her alone, alone!

Moon and star in wild eclipse
Reel at the meeting of our lips.

Her hair falls free,—her beauteous face
Puts a charm on the common place:

Down in the depths of my yearning eyes,
A common nature grows pure and wise.

Shapes of wonder and beauty stray
O'er the place and the heart that are poor by day!

Down, O sun! arise, O moon!
That the magic may come upon us soon.

Die, O day! come, eventide!
That the common things may be beautified.

Come, and go not soon away!
We dwindle again in the garish day!

Rise, O moon, upon the place,
Whiten the wonder on her face!

Come, O Love, to my red heart's core,
Lighten and purify me more!

SAILOR'S LOVE.

WHAT should I look on as I went aboard ship,
    But lovers quarrelling down along the dale?
Quiet and sly and sneering was his lordship,
    The lass looked greener than a dolphin's tail.
'Heigho!' cried I, 'this comes of love on land;
    Too much of company brings pain and smarting,—
A romp among the pretty ones is grand;
    Sweet greeting, though, for me, and speedy parting.'

Inez is smiling, if you call at Cadiz;
    Drop down by Wapping, there grins English Sue;
All the world o'er, the pretty smiling ladies
    Wait for the sailor, always trim and true;
Merry for ever, always fresh and free,
    Sorry a little when we talk of starting,
But never grudging one his libertie;
    Sweet greeting, then, say I, and speedy parting.

Can't tie a lad and lass like logs together,
    But they must bore each other now and then;
One can't be smiling in all sorts of weather,—
    Women are women only, men are men.

After the days afloat, a day ashore,
  Glad welcome from the pretty faces darting;
A kiss—a dance—then, hey! away once more;—
  Sweet greeting, then, say I, and speedy parting.

Pleasant the pretty prattling and beguiling,
  After a busy dashing up and down;
Sun, lads, a little, in a woman's smiling,
  But go aboard ere she has time to frown;
And coming ever pleasant, ever new,
  See nothing of the fretting and the smarting,
But find the fair ones ever kind and true:
  Sweet greeting, then, say I, and speedy parting.

'WHICH WOULD YOU KISS?'

Which would you kiss? A cheek like this,
    Ruddy and ripe and mellow,
Or the languid and mild cheek of the child
    Of some well-acred fellow?

And how would you kiss? For a cheek like this,
    A tasty smack and rare!
But daintily brush o'er the languid blush,
    When you kiss the lady fair.

Which would you choose to be your Muse?
    To whom would you say or sigh love?
Which of the two is the mate for you,—
    The lowly or the high love?
Oh, daintily kiss your high-born miss,
    Till ye scorn, or die, or sever;
While roundly I kiss a cheek like this,
    And find it fond for ever!

MOTHER RUMOUR.

WHAT did Mother Rumour do?
Over the whole wide world she flew,
Upsetting kings, reversing laws,
In her state coach drawn by pies and daws.

MOTHER RUMOUR.

A speaking-trumpet in her hand,
She cried aloud thro' every land;
English, Spanish, Turkish, Greek—
Every tongue the witch could speak.

Everywhere her notes were heard,
By man and woman, beast and bird:
Such a babble in the air!
'T was chatter, chatter, everywhere!—

From the Sultan's bright seraglio,
Where languid trouser'd beauties blow,
To Goody Blake and Goody Blane
Gossiping in an English lane.

Little king or queen could do
But noisy Mother Rumour knew;
Not a thing, however small,
But she was warned about it all:

Terrible things and wicked things,
Court and cottage whisperings,
Shrieks of pain and cries of power,
Cooings from my lady's bower.

Kings and courtiers saw her pass,
Pretty sinners cried 'Alas!'
Treason hunched his back,—while she
Doomed him to the gallows-tree.

MOTHER RUMOUR.

The murderer, as he turned to fly,
Shrieked to hear her dreadful cry,
And tore his hair :—for as he flew,
All the pallid people knew!

Two magpies, sitting on a fir,
Croaked chuckling, as they looked at her,
'What a world the world must be,
Ruled by such a witch as she!'

But the lark went up to Heaven's gate,
And sang his ditty early and late—
'Hither, hither!' was his cry,
'The witch can never soar as high!'

WHERE THE WIND COMES FRAE.

OH weel I mind, Oh weel I mind,
  Tho' now my locks are snaw,
How oft langsyne I sought to find
  What made the bellows blaw!
How, cuddling on my grannie's knee,
  I questioned night and day,
And still the thing that puzzled me
  Was—where the wind came frae?

Tho' I hae dwelt for many a year
  Thro' pleasure and thro' pain,
Still must I rax my wits and speir,
  And wish the puzzle plain?
The warld o' men wi' change on change
  Rolls darkly on its way,
And still I ask, in wonder strange,
  Where, where the wind comes frae?

The wind that beats the widow's face
  Outside the rich man's door,
The wind that drives the human race,
  And levels rich and poor;

The wind that breaks a people's chain,
  Or doth a monarch slay,—
While weary men in doubt or pain
  Ask—where the wind comes frae?

Oh, I hae striven, loved, and sinned,
  And I hae lost in tears,
But now the hollow eerie Wind
  Sounds sweeter in mine ears.
Depart, O life! come soon, O death!
  Till I am blest as they,
Who, brightening beneath His breath,
  Wake—where the wind comes frae!

90

PEACE.

WAR thunders out of other lands,
And men are slain by human hands,
And mothers' moans and widows' tears
Sadden the sweetness of the years.

But here in England blooms the palm,
Is breathed the prayer and sung the psalm;
Though, sleepless on his iron height,
The Lion's eye is rolled in light.

The stream unreddened sweeps along;
The poet hums a quiet song;
Yet, from the anvil's piercing tongue
The war-cry of the sword is rung.

In English meadows sleeps the lamb,
Meek symbol of the pure 'I AM';
But dark in yon celestial sky
A taloned Fate is sailing by.

But keep, O England, peaceful rule;
Far from thy shores be knave and fool;
Lest the slow anger of thy sons
Loose the swift lightning of their guns.

And pour, O God, around this isle
The living splendour of Thy smile,
That all our bays and peaks may be
Havens and thrones of Liberty!

DALZIEL BROTHERS
ENGRAVERS & PRINTERS

Camden
Press

www.ingramcontent.com/pod-product-compliance
Lightning Source LLC
Chambersburg PA
CBHW030549040726
47497CB00008B/2634